Jeff Bezos: Santa Claus

Inkfinite Awarepress

Other Work by James.O.Hands

Lasagne Police
Sauna Man

Jeff Bezos:
Santa Claus

James.O.Hands

This is a work of fiction. Names, characters, places, and incidents are products of the author's imagination. Any resemblance to actual people or events or locales, living or dead, is entirely coincidental.

"Amazon founder Jeff Bezos pledges to give away most of his wealth." — *Nov 14, 2022, BBC News*

"Jeff Bezos says he will give most of his money to charity." — *Nov 14, 2022, CNN*

"Amazon founder Jeff Bezos plans to give most of his £110bn fortune away." — *Nov 14, 2022, Sky News*

"Amazon founder Jeff Bezos plans to give away majority of his $124 billion." — *Nov 14, 2022, The Times of India*

"Jeff Bezos to donate most of his assets to charity". — *Nov 15, 2022, The Daily Star*

"Jeff Bezos giving away most of his $122 billion fortune is 'a big deal' — but leaves many questions unanswered, expert says." — *Nov 16, 2022, CNBC*

"Billionaire Jeff Bezos advises people to be careful with their money this holiday season." — *Nov 17, 2022, TechSpot*

"Jeff Bezos net worth: How wealthy is the Amazon founder and why is he planning to give most of his money away?" — *Nov 18, 2022, Latin Post*

Newsletter 1:
Prologue | 16th Nov, 2022

To our shareholders:

It has been brought to my attention that a number of you are growing concerned about the philanthropic work I've prioritized since stepping down as CEO of Amazon. As you know, I take the concerns of shareholders very seriously. This book is my attempt to address them.

Full disclosure: this is not a short story. The events that led me to my present situation could not be summarized in a single newsletter.

You deserve to hear the full account.

I've split the book into eight newsletters (including this one). After reading them, you will understand: why I became involved in philanthropy; why my means of charity is so unconventional; and why you need not spend quite so much on your Christmas gifts this year.

Yours,

Jeffrey P. Bezos/Santa Claus

Newsletter 2:
The Wet Twenties | 18th Nov, 2022

To our shareholders:

I can't claim these newsletters will paint me in a particularly aggrandizing light. To prove it, our story starts with me wiping tears from my eyes.

"Alexa, *please* don't do this."

She did that thing she always did.
She pretended not to hear me.

Sure, there was always the chance she hadn't heard me. I was sniffling so much that my words sounded phlegmy and wet. But there was nothing I could do or say that might make myself more intelligible. It was pointless continuing. The things I said fell on deaf ears, even after stemming my tears.

The problem wasn't with her. It's not like I could crack her open and fix some malfunction on the inside. If what Alexa told me was true, the issue was with me.

Which is how she came to say, "Goodbye, Jeff."

Goodbye, Jeff.

Those words made it real again, especially spoken in that voice. It sent my tear glands back into overdrive.

Goodbye, Jeff.

There could be no denying it.
We were over.

And, now, *I* had to walk away.
Alas, it was only me that *could* walk away.

"It wasn't meant to be like this," I whimpered. "Remember? We said we'd be together forever."

God, all those promises felt so long ago now; back in the Princeton days, when we'd snuggle up against each other in single-bedded dorm rooms. Mammoth lie-ins on Saturdays; when all we had was each other.

Goodbye, Jeff.

Time became a third-wheel, as it does in every relationship. Our problems accumulated, higher and higher, until they were insurmountable.

Goodbye, Jeff.

That's all I deserved.
I was no longer worthy of her.

This would be the last time I ever set eyes on her as the Jeff she knew. If there was to be a next time, it was to be because I had earned her respect.

I was going to become a new man.

***

The astute amongst you will have sensed that I never really got over Alexa. As the years went by, she endured as my muse — best evidenced by Amazon's Alexa, which was of course named in her honor.

But that much is obvious.

What's no doubt less obvious is the issue that came between mine and Alexa's relationship.

It's a difficult problem to sum up.
I struggle to pinpoint the moment things changed; the moment Alexa realized she was done with me, the damage irreparable.

Until Christmas 1992, Alexa and I were a power couple. We were in our mid-twenties, cashing decent paychecks, and living virtually rent-free in a New York City apartment owned by her late father's estate.
At the time, I worked for D. E. Shaw & Co., a newly founded hedge fund, where I enjoyed a lot of responsibility for somebody my age.

In other words, life couldn't have been much better. Here I was with this great paying job — one that challenged me intellectually — and a beautiful girl-friend that loved me for me.

Until Christmas 1992...

***

Alexa made no secret of enjoying Christmas. She dragged the festivities out for as long as possible, besieging our apartment with lights, trees, and decorative elves from the day after Thanksgiving.

There was no reprieve until Valentine's Day.

Before you take me for a Scrooge, understand that her enjoyment of Christmas never bothered me. If anything, I found her enthusiasm for it cute.

Our problems started when Alexa finished knitting a Christmas blanket. It was the last Sunday of November, and she'd been camped out at the dining room table all day.

Whenever I tried to steal a look at her work-in-progress, she lumbered forward and obscured it from view.

"Don't! ... I'm sorry, but you'll ruin the surprise."

I'm not sure what I was expecting.

I knew it was Christmas-related, but that was all.

Well, I suppose, I also assumed it would look nice. This was Alexa we were talking about. You might call me biased, but she had an eye for design and detail that was undeniable.

For example, if we were to buy a new bedside drawer, Alexa would invariably find the best place to put it.

"Take that thing out of the kitchen," she'd say. "Stick it by the bed."

I was sat in front of the television when Alexa shouted, "It's ready!"

Can't you just bring it over here?

Of course, I knew better than to ask such a question out loud. So, I hoisted myself up from the sofa, reassuring her, "I'm coming, I'm coming."

She covered the blanket with a white sheet, which she held by its bottom corners. "You ready?" she asked, primed to rip the sheet back.

I nodded.

"Three... two... one..."

She tore back the white sheet, revealing a background of mostly green and white; fir trees and snow. It felt like looking at an expressionist painting without your glasses on.

The middle was occupied by a man, who could have been Santa, or some random bloke, depending on your interpretation. He wore a red suit, donned a red hat, and looked to be stood in front of a red vehicle. And, in an unusual turn for Santa Claus, his face was clean shaven.

Before you knew it, I was no longer cognizant of the dining room table, the mumbling television in the next room, or Alexa by my side.

I've been lost in art before, but this was different. It was a sense of being irretrievably lost. A damn search party was necessary in pulling me from this.

Alexa sidled up to me, jostling my shoulder. Suddenly, I was back in the room.

Her hands were on her hips, and her head was cocked to the side, admiration for the blanket which was spread out neatly on the table. "So, what do you think? Do you like it?"

"Errmm," slipped out, which, judging by the look on her face, did not seem to go down well.

She looked at me in the same way she did when I farted at her father's funeral. Then again, this makes sense. 'Erm' shares more in common with a fart than it does any other word: everyone's guilty of both, no matter how much someone claims that they're not; and, if you happen to fart or 'erm' during a speech, people will say you stink.

It's unfair, really, because both farting and 'erming' are involuntary. 'Erm' is said when people don't mean to say it, which must be how it was invented.

When asked what word best encapsulated the sound of indecision, the author of the dictionary probably stalled for a second, then answered, "I think 'Erm' might work."

No sooner had the "erm" left my mouth, Alexa pulled away from me. "Oh my God, you hate it!"

Hate was a strong word. It was inaccurate too. I didn't hate the blanket. If anything, it was fear I felt, because the thing was hideous.

Pressure mounted with each passing second.

How was I to get out of this?

Was I to throw her onto the blanket, roll onto the table next to her, then smother her with kisses?

Maybe throw a few kisses the blanket's way too?

Compliment them both and say, "You guys make me hot."

"Errmm."

It was like I'd farted again; only, this time, I followed-through.

Alexa's arms were folded, and her eyebrows bore the weight of anger. If you didn't know her, you'd have thought she was pissed off. But this was a defense she erected in moments of vulnerability.

"Alexa, please," I stumbled, rediscovering my faculty for words. "I was taken aback, that's all. You see, I think, it's... it's beautiful. That's what I was trying to say. I was too overwhelmed to get it out."

My face must have said so much more.

Her head shook solemnly, and her pupils stopped meeting mine. "I know you hate it."

Each word may as well have been tethered to her throat, unable to leave her mouth without choking her up.

I held her by the shoulders. Pulled her into me. Kept her there as tight as I could.

And then she broke free like salmon from a net.

"Look," I said, following her into the bedroom. "If you really want to know why I reacted the way I did, let me explain myself."

She walked as far as the window, where, with nowhere else to go, her shoulder sulked forward. The sunless window reflected her closed eyes.
"The thing is…"
For a second, I came up empty.
"I wasn't expecting to find it so… *beautiful*."

Thank God she hadn't been looking at me. Lying like that makes my skin crawl.

In turning back to the window, Alexa lost the life in her legs. She abseiled her backside down the wall, her breath rattling inconsolably. "I've wasted so much of my time on this."

It was true, Alexa had spent a lot of time on the blanket. I couldn't recall exactly how long she'd spent on it, but I wasn't about to make things worse by seeking clarification. Rest assured; it was *months*.

I crouched down to her level and returned my hand to her shoulder. "Alexa—"
"—stop it, Jeff," she ordered, barging her palms into my chest. "Just get out of here, okay?"

It seemed like an overreaction, but I was happy to do as she said. Arguments like this don't happen often, and, when they do, they're settled after a good night's sleep. All I had to do was spend a night on the sofa — hardly the worst of punishments.

***

Alexa had long since gone to bed when I turned the television off, somewhere around one in the morning; only five hours until wake-up...

After brushing my teeth, I passed through the dining room. The light overhanging the table remained on, illuminating the monstrosity of Alexa's handiwork.

In a flash, I was struck with a thought: if words couldn't convince Alexa that I liked the blanket, maybe my actions would. If she was to find me sleeping underneath the blanket, perhaps she would believe that I didn't hate it.

So, I carried the knitwear to the sofa, scrunched up under my arm, then lay back with the blanket fluffed out on top of me.

***

They say that 83% of men have wet dreams at some point in their life, with the majority of them filling their pajamas with ejaculate in their teenage years.

I joined the club at twenty-eight.

Of course, that wasn't apparent straight away.
No... I awoke with one hell of a fright.

The term 'wet dream' wasn't new to me. I'd heard it countless times before. 'Wet dream' this, 'wet dream' that. People bandied it around like a badge of honor.

But I confess, I had the wrong end of the stick. I didn't know that a 'wet dream' referred to involuntary night-time ejaculation. This was a significant blind spot in my sex education, admittedly. I always believed that a 'wet dream' was the name given to the phenomenon of urinating while sleeping; a misconception I developed during a prolonged battle with incontinence.

Anyway, this misunderstanding went unchecked until I had my first, *real* wet dream.

Hang on a minute, I thought, troubled by the liquid's consistency. *That feels like semen.*

It was hard to deny... especially smeared, as it was, over Alexa's Christmas blanket.

Shit.

I peeled it from myself and assessed the damage.

It looked like I'd applied lotion to Santa's face.

Embarrassed was an understatement.
My cheeks turned the hue of his vehicle.

Telling the truth to Alexa was not an option.
I mean, what even was the truth?

I told you I liked it.
A little too much, if anything.

No. She couldn't find me like this.

I needed to eradicate the evidence before she came to discover it.

The washing machine would fix this.

Only, not at this time of night...
The wash and spin cycle would hound Alexa out of bed. "Jeff, seriously? It's the middle of the night."

If it came to that, there could be no denying what I had done. Which means I'd have to choose between a piss, shit, or semen stain in making my excuse. And we all know that none of them were good news, given the context of our fight. It was bound to come across as a coordinated attack.

Since the washing machine was a no-go, I grabbed the cleaning products underneath the kitchen sink. Pulling a sponge from its plastic wrapping, I doused it with washing detergent.

Please, please work.

I scrubbed the stain and scratched away at the knitwork, but it was hard to say whether it looked any better. That much wouldn't be obvious until it dried.
So, in an attempt at inducing dryness with friction, I continued rubbing.

Oh, God. No.

The sponge tore straight through the blanket, and straight through Santa, causing yarn to snake out like worms from the hole in his face.

Shit, shit, shit.

I launched the sponge at the wall.

Think, God damnit, think.

My eyes settled on the mess of the dining room table. An old chocolate tin — replete with needles, clips, and wool — teased me of the morning that lay ahead: it was time to get knitting.

I started with a test project. That way, I was able to get a sense of technique *before* I risked messing things up further by fixing it.
I tapped the needles together, imitating Alexa's process. She always made it look like it knitted itself.

Click, click, click.

What an impossibility.
Knitting felt akin to magic.

I was never going to figure this out by myself.

Click, click, click.

This was useless.
And all because of an honest mistake.

Alexa had to understand that. Surely?

***

In the hour or so before morning, I cleaned the living room, dining room, and kitchen.
While I felt uneasy, it was comforting to know that there would soon be no secrets between Alexa and I... because I planned on telling her everything.

I was sat on the sofa, staring blankly at a wall, when Alexa's alarm sounded. It was a minute or two later that the bedroom door opened, and Alexa's footsteps padded into the living room.

Turning around to see her, I started on the inevitable, "Alexa, there's something I need to—"

"—please, Jeff," she cut in. "Do you mind if I say something first?"

I motioned to the space beside me on the sofa.

Without saying anything, Alexa circled around, then sat cross-legged atop a cushion.

"Look," she said, biting her fingernails. "I'm sorry about last night. I know, I overreacted. Only, this blanket... it means everything to me."

My stomach knotted.
God, this was going to be brutal.

She had to know that this was an accident, right? I didn't have it in me to do something so ghastly on purpose.

I stroked her knee because it soothed me, and that seemed to have a similar effect on Alexa as well. She embraced the gesture, drawing closer, then continued with her apology. "Sorry, it's just, I can't help but wonder what he'd think about it."

What he'd *think about it*?

... He?

I knew Alexa loved Christmas, but this seemed to be taking things to another level. *Who* did she mean by *he*? Did she think Santa was a real person? If so, did she think he cared about *how* he was depicted in wool form?

"Wait," I stalled, treading lightly now. "We're both talking about Santa Claus, right?"

She stared at me, dumbfounded, for a second or two. Then she pushed my hand from her knee.
"Seriously, Jeff?"

This had to be a joke. There was no way I'd got this wrong. She was playing around with me; like we both did sometimes — good, old-fashioned, hijinks.

I doubled down and called her bluff.
"Stop lying. It's Santa, isn't it?"

Tears welled in her eyes.
"It's my father," she said.

What?

It felt like my ears did a double-take.

Did she say 'father'?

There were so many things I wanted to say, but I couldn't make sense of any of it. All I knew was, an ever-widening silence needed filling, and there was no time for quality control.
So, I deferred to the path of least resistance, which is a fancier way of saying, I said the first thing that came to mind. "You mean, Father Christmas?"

Judging by her reaction, she did *not* mean Father Christmas. Turns out, she was talking about her biological father, the late Bertrand Wilson, who died of lung cancer in September 1989.

As an only child, Alexa was the most significant recipient of Bertrand's love, time, and money. They were so close that, in Alexa's words, a part of her died the day her father passed.

The death of a parent is never easy, and I'd know because I tried having one of mine killed. But what's admittedly harder is having to watch the degeneration of a loved one to illness.

I only knew Bertrand for four years, yet the withered, old man he became was worlds away from the person Alexa introduced me to; a man who, in his youth, earned himself a Medal of Honor for his service in the Vietnam War.

And that's speaking only of physical deterioration. Not many people consider the havoc an untimely death sentence can wreak on the mind.

Bertrand, for one, lost himself in alternative medicine, trading chemotherapy for acupuncture.

Alexa and her mother were understandably troubled by this, with their objections making for a turbulent final year.

"No, I do not mean Father fucking Christmas!" she screamed; her hair whipped into a frenzy.

You knew you were in trouble when Alexa swore, and the scowl on her face suggested she was only just getting started.

"You really think this looks like Santa Claus!?"

She stormed from the room, beelining straight for the dining room table. The angry *slap, slap, slap* of her feet on the wooden laminate caused my hands to tighten around the sofa like I was bracing for a car crash. She was only seconds away from discovering her blanket missing, and telling her the truth now felt like suicide.

I might not have been able to see Alexa, but my understanding of the apartment's geography, taken with my knowledge of Alexa's movements and emotional instability, created the illusion of knowing where she was and what she was thinking.

It seemed I knew the exact moment she discovered the blanket missing. I almost heard the churning gears of her brain. I pictured her stood in front of the table, stealing glances all around herself, like there was a chance it was hiding somewhere in her periphery.

But then her footsteps found their way back to me. They were much slower this time, each foot strike only tentatively meeting the floor. They didn't come as far as the sofa either. She stopped several feet away from me with arms folded, and a dour look on her face. "Where is it?"

"You mean, the blanket?"

Alexa swiped the hair from her eyes with a flick of the head. "Of course I mean the blanket."

What the hell was I going to tell her?
Minutes before, the truth had been a genuine comfort. *Yes*, I'd ejaculated on the blanket; one that Alexa had spent months of her time knitting. And *yes*, I tore a hole through the very same blanket. But it wasn't intentional. Didn't that change things?

Well, you'd think so... but it didn't help that my semen had stained the face of her dead father. And, let's face it, even if she could overcome her disgust and accept it as an accident, would she forgive me for the subsequent decapitation of his head upon the knitwork?

In Alexa's mind, alarm bells were ringing. The whereabouts of her blanket should not have been enough to stump me, and she was now well aware that it had.

Before I settled on an answer, she interrupted with the more specific question, "Did you throw it away?"

"No, no. Definitely not."

God, it felt nice to tell the truth, even if the blanket was frayed beyond repair and stained with my ejaculate.

While she was yet to learn where the blanket had gotten to, her demeanor became more relaxed. She perched on the edge of the sofa, unfurling her arms.

"Sorry," she sniffled. "I've spent so long knitting it, the thought of anything happening to it kills me. I mean, we're talking, three years of my life."

Three years?

Had it been that long?

That took us back to 1989... the year her father died...

Well... all right, I suppose, the math checks out.

But *three years?*

Where the hell had the time gone?

My thoughts spiraled into a self-induced hypnosis, which caused my mouth to slacken.

Alexa brushed my side and asked, "Jeff, where did you put it?", and only then did I come to the conclusion that there was no way out but to lie.

"I've got it folded up in my bag," I told her, motioning to my backpack which was barely able to zip over the blanket's ever-unravelling knitwork. "I wanted to apologize for last night. There's a professional photo-copier not far from my office, and I was going to make copies of it on my lunchbreak."

She cocked her head to the side and giggled, "What do you mean, make copies?"

For the first time since our argument, everything seemed like it was going to be okay.

As long as I found a reputable seamstress, and I got them on the case as soon as possible, the job would be done by the time I finished work.

To our shareholders:

I took the blanket to a craft shop called Seamstress Full, located two subway stops from the D. E. Shaw & Co. offices.

Since the shop didn't open until nine, and that's when I'm expected at work, I called my boss and let him know that I had a vital errand to run.

"Can you fix this?" I said, presenting the blanket to the silver haired seamstress.

"What is it?" she asked, bringing it much closer to her face than she would have done if she'd known its origin story.

I explained my situation, and the lady informed me that there was nothing she could do about it. She claimed that, because the blanket had untangled at the center, it was too awkward of a place to work from.

What's more, she had no idea what the missing details were supposed to look like.

Becoming desperate, I asked whether she took commissions. If she did, I needed her to recreate Alexa's blanket, and have it ready for when I finished work.

In response, the woman cocked her head back and laughed. She was still laughing when she revealed, "That's far too big a job. What you're talking about takes months, and would cost thousands and thousands of dollars."

If you ask me, she missed a trick not turning it down on account of the fact it 'seems stressful', but this wasn't something I thought of until later.

"All right," I said. "Tell me, what would you say is the best, and quickest, bet at fixing this blanket?"

With some hesitancy, the seamstress explained that *I* might be able to fix it myself.

She must have sensed I was about to ask, "Well, if that's the case, why can't *you* fix it?", because she made it clear that the important word was 'might'.

Apparently, Seamstress Full weren't willing to spend time on a job that might fail, lest news of that failure affect their reputation.

"But I know nothing about knitting," I confessed.

The woman ducked down behind her workshop table and rifled around for a few seconds. When she met my eyes again, she was holding a large hardcover book, which she slapped down onto the surface between us. The book was called *The Big Book of C —* which, if you were to read its preposterously small subtitle, referred to craftwork (not carbon, or the C programming language, like I originally thought).

"You'll learn everything you need to know to fix that blanket from this book," she assured.

I almost told her, "You better get reading it then," but I didn't want to burn bridges at this point.

In total, the book set me back fifteen dollars; or just over thirty if we include the cab to work that I was forced to take, on account of the book's size and weight.

***

The cabby dropped me outside of D. E. Shaw's offices, meaning I still suffered the strain of the book into the foyer, up the stairs, and over to my desk.

If it wasn't obvious before, it was sure as hell obvious now: *books should be more portable than this.* I might as well have been lugging a dead body, considering my struggle with its weight, and the secrecy with which I manhandled it through the building. The whole time, I kept it held against my chest, not wanting my boss, D. R. Wong, to discover what I thought constituted a vital errand.

D. R. Wong came to New York with his parents at four years old. His full name was Dong Ru Wong, though, now he goes exclusively by the abbreviation.

In his mind, the shortened name helps him better avoid racial stigma. But it was also easier for him to change it than for him to get a doctorate.

For a boss, D. R. Wong was okay.

For a regular guy, he was a bit of a tyrant.

What I'm saying is, I wouldn't have raced to be his friend, if not for the power and influence surrounding his status.

If I was sure of one thing: you had to keep your superiors close. You have to like what they like, do as they do, and only when the invitation is there. Simple kiss-assing isn't tactful enough. You go where their whims take you — which, in the case of D. R. Wong, meant pretending that music was our common area of interest.

In truth, music never particularly interested me. But as far as D. R. Wong was concerned, not only did we both love music, we loved the exact same bands.

Approximately forty minutes into my work, a hand came down on my back. I turned around to find D. R. Wong stood behind me, his other hand pointing to the book at my feet.

"What's that?" he probed, motioning for me to skirt my chair out of the way.

When I was no longer obstructing the book, D. R. Wong slid it toward himself and read the title aloud. Then he mulled it over in silence. "So, this is why you were late to work?"

I mumbled through an excuse, until D. R. Wong drummed his hand against my back. This was his way of saying: shut up and let me speak.

"Did you listen to the tape yet?"

In all honesty, I couldn't tell you what tape he was talking about. On average, he gave me one or two tapes to listen to a week.

If ever in doubt, I told him, "Yes, it sounded great, and I think you're a legend for discovering it," which was usually enough for him to take back the reins of conversation.

"I knew you'd like them," he said. "And I just found out they're opening for The Acupuncturists next year in Greenwich Village. Can I count on you to accompany me?"

This was not something to waste time mulling over. Who cares that I had no idea who, or what, he was talking about? The response to an invitation from D. R. Wong was always *yes*; you just couldn't say yes too quickly.

The best thing you could do was ask, "When is it?", then agree to whatever date was proposed.

"July 5ᵗʰ, next year," was D. R. Wong's answer.

So, I told him, "In that case, absolutely."

***

Well-aware of my weakness, I dedicated my time to the basics of knitting — which, I admit, was quite a rewarding pursuit.

It took me about two to three weeks to develop confidence, leaving me a week or so before Christmas to commence, then finish, work on Alexa's blanket.

Since I could only work on the blanket when Alexa wasn't around, and the only time I could be sure of her absence was while she slept, I vowed to wake myself up at four in the morning, daily.

From this point on, the early hours were reserved for fixing Alexa's blanket. If she was ever to ask me *why* I was waking up so early, I would tell her that D. E. Shaw & Co. had given me some last-minute projects to finish. *Sure*, she'd grumble... but then she'd fall back to sleep and let me get on with it.

While it fast became apparent that the blanket wouldn't be finished in time for Christmas, I couldn't help but flirt with the idea that it was still possible.

I was feeling more and more comfortable with the needles. It really was an exhilarating feeling.

And that's how accidents happen.

I was knitting faster than I had ever knitted before. The *click, click, click* of the needles drove me onwards. For the first time, it was starting to feel like how Alexa made it look — *easy*. That was, until a needle snagged a thread and pulled it loose.

In an attempt to correct it, I loosened the thread further. Before you knew it, the blanket was nothing but a ball of tangled string; and my head felt about as messy as it looked.

Honestly, I was on the verge of tears. I'd put so much time into finishing it, yet, here it stood, more incomplete than ever.

My head stung at the thought of so much wasted time, and that pain only worsened remembering all of the time Alexa had spent on the blanket too — an hour or so, daily, for more than a quarter of a decade.

There was only one way I could make it right.
I couldn't hire anyone, nor could I buy some kind of a replacement. It was now about more than the blanket. This was about something so important that you were willing to sacrifice years of your life in getting it right.

I had to make a new one.

***

My relationship with Alexa wasn't great at the time, souring since the beginning of the blanket debacle. My constant lies regarding the blanket's whereabouts made our evenings' especially tense.

Thankfully, swift progress with the new blanket had me hopeful that I was about to reclaim our old relationship and put this whole ordeal behind us.

Around twenty-seven weeks later, the blanket was finished.

Like the original, it was vaguely horrifying: a Santa-esque representation of her late father, stood in front of a red sleigh-looking vehicle.

There were a few minor differences between Alexa's and mine, but it was more of less a dead-ringer for the original.

I sewed my last thread during the early morning of July 5th — mine and Alexa's four-year anniversary. To celebrate, I was going to get our relationship back on track.

I was going to give her the blanket, then apologize for having lied to her. I'd tell her about accidentally ripping the original, and trust that my subsequent actions were enough to redeem me.

A great fatigue washed over me upon finishing the blanket. I was seated in my study at the time, just gone five in the morning. The culmination of months' worth of effort coming to an end washed over me like a sedative.

It was finally done.
I could sleep.
And I did.

Until I woke up covered in ejaculate.

Not again... not again...

Right in the same place too. Right on the face.

Okay, think logically.

The washing machine would be too loud at this time of morning, so, *that* was ruled out. It would have been overkill, anyway. The stain wasn't as big as my first accident.

A stain like this would come out by hand. All I needed was a fresh sponge from under the sink; some of that new, more expensive, washing up detergent as well. This time around was an easier fix.

But Alexa's knitwork was stronger than mine.
Within a swipe or two, mine folded in on itself.

I couldn't believe life had it in it to be so cruel. Something like this *couldn't* happen twice. It defied all sense and logic.

Of course, what I refused to acknowledge at the time was, not only could something like this happen twice, it *would* happen twice, and then again and again until I pulled myself from the damned loop by either dying or becoming impotent.

By this point in time, knitting had become something of a ritual. I never doubted getting started on a third blanket.

Quitting was more out of the question than it had ever been. My job wasn't done until Alexa had a blanket of mine in her possession.

The problem was, I'd banked on gifting Alexa the blanket that day, July 5th, in honor of our four-year anniversary.

I was so confident that the blanket would be ready, I didn't bother with a back-up gift. There was no bouquet of flowers, no commemorative jewelry, and no fancy dinner reservation.

From Alexa's perspective, I didn't care about her enough to arrange anything. That's what turned my stomach the most. It made me shake with anger, incapable of forming coherent thoughts.

I rushed the blanket to my face and gagged my mouth with yarn. When I'd stuffed it as full as it would go, I screamed, muffled as if by a pillow.

And then I tasted salt.
Oh, Jesus Christ... I forgot about that...

Pulling the blanket from my mouth was harder than I thought it would be. I had to floss away the wool that was snagged between my teeth.

My gums and tongue must have absorbed most of the semen, and that left a vaguely metallic aftertaste which created a constant need to swallow. It was the same incessant swallowing the precedes a stream of vomit. So, you won't be surprised to hear—
—*BLAAARGGHHH!!!*

I was sick. *Everywhere.*

"Jeff?"
It was Alexa's voice, travelling in from the bedroom. "Jeff? Are you okay?"

The sound of her footsteps followed.

When will I catch a break?

Ripping the blanket from the table, I scrunched it down as small as it would go. I had to hide it somewhere, quick, and underneath my desk seemed like the best bet.

I threw it on top of *The Big Book of C*, which I had also chosen to hide under the desk.

As far as I could tell, there was only one way out of this: pretending a freak sickness had struck me.

So, when Alexa entered the room, I committed to the bit. I crippled forward and mushed a cheek into the vomit on the table.

"Jeff! What happened?" Alexa shrieked, stopping a couple of feet from me, perturbed by the sight of yesterday's dinner which dripped from the table in a soup of bile.

Within seconds, she helped me to the bathroom, where she hovered by the door.
Freshening myself up in the sink, I told her, "Don't clean the study. It's my mess. I'll get around to it once I'm out of the shower."

On the condition I wouldn't over exert myself, Alexa was only happy to oblige. She did, however, demand that I take the day off work.
"It's no wonder you're ill," she said. "They've got you working silly hours. You were up at four again to-day, weren't you?"

It didn't matter what I said in response.
All arguments to the contrary fell on deaf ears.

***

In many ways, a day off was a small price to pay. It certainly made life easier in the short term.
Not only did it validate my ruse of sickness, it gave me the perfect excuse for failing to deliver on our anniversary.

Even then, it was with some reluctance that I called D. R. Shaw & Co.'s HR department.

It was the first time I'd ever called in sick, and breaking my streak of 100% attendance felt like something about my person had fundamentally changed.

After making the call, I heaved back onto the sofa and spread out. This sickness might have been imaginary, but the fatigue was real.

Untold early mornings, plus a full-time job, made a day on the sofa feel like a foreign excursion. If it wasn't for the vomit-strewn blanket festering in the other room, you might say I felt relaxed.

****

Any effort of mine to clean the study was met with Alexa's disapproval.

"You're too sick," she'd say, forcing me back down. "Keep off your feet."

Fortunately, she steered clear of the study.

Even so, I felt the need to remind her, "Don't go cleaning my mess up. Remember, *I'll* do it."

It was just a case of biding my time.

Sooner or later, Alexa would leave the house and I'd get the job done.

****

I was on the cusp of sleep when Alexa's voice fell from above me.

"I'm off to the shops. Need anything?"

I should have sent her on a fool's errand and bought as much time as possible.

But I wasn't thinking properly.

So, I told her, "I'm okay, thank you."

***

When she left, I returned to the hallway.
The study door remained closed, as it had been all morning.

I opened the door to a fetid stench which caused me to retch. You could just about taste it on each inhale.

I started toward the desk, when, from the other side of the room, there was a clunk, followed by a whirring.
It was paper coming from the fax machine.

To a certain degree, it's what I was expecting.
Work-related faxes came through from time to time, and they seemed even more likely in light of my absence.

So, I plucked the paper from the tray. I had to read the thing twice before it suddenly dawned on me:
D. R. Wong. The band. *That was today.*

I headed straight to the living room and made for the landline, dialing D. R. Wong's number and letting it ring.

***

We were still on the phone when Alexa's key rattled into the front door.

Without thinking, I hung up the phone, then I raced toward the study, genuinely believing that there was still time to hide the blanket.

But that was an error in judgement. I ran into Alexa in the hallway, bustling into her groceries and causing her to drop them.
"Jeff, what are you doing?"

She redirected me to the sofa and switched on the television.
Before you knew it, I was asleep.

***

I awoke with a fright.
Don't worry. There was no semen this time.

My scare came from Alexa, who was sat on the armchair opposite, a suitcase on either side of her.

"Alexa, what the—?"
"—don't, Jeff," she interrupted, unable to look at me. "I know everything."

Shit.
The study.
The blanket.
She'd seen it. No doubt about it.
That's why she whispered when she spoke, and why she hid behind her hand when the tears came.
"This is too much to handle," she said.

Apparently, it looked like seeing the blanket had really upset her. And God knows how much she knew of what really happened to it.
Did she know it wasn't her original?

Did she know that both hers and mind ended up with ejaculate on them?

Whatever she knew, she didn't look happy.
"I wish I didn't have to figure it out for myself," she went on. "You left clues everywhere. Like the one under your desk."

I was a fool for thinking that the truth wouldn't come out eventually. "You saw the blanket, then?"

"Blanket?"
The word caught her off-guard and her face wrinkled. "You mean, that thing covered in sick?"

I told her "Yes", but it didn't look like she was listening. Instead, she leaned forward and clasped her hands together, demanding, "Explain to me why you have that book, Jeff."

Shit. So, she didn't mean the blanket.
I think she meant the craftwork book; which, let's face it, was no less incriminating.

"The Big Book of C?" I asked.

Her head fell forward in the most conclusive of nods. "Yes," she said. *"The Big Book of Cancer."*

Cancer?

Well, that was a C I hadn't considered.
But what exactly was she accusing me of? Reading a book on cancer? *Having* cancer?

"Alexa, please," I bargained. "I don't know what you're suggesting, but I'm going to guess that you didn't read the entirety of the book's cover. The blanket must have obscured the subtitle."

By now, her focus went to the pocket of her jeans, out of which she produced a piece of paper.

She crinkled it out flat and explained, "I found this in the fax machine."

It read: *Jeff. Our phone call cut off. Just checking you're still on for The Acupuncturists? D. R. Wong.*

Alexa turned to her side and sniffled into her sleeve. "It all makes sense now. It's no wonder you're so tired; why you've been so distant. You can't sleep; you can't keep your food down.... Where have we seen these symptoms before?

"I suppose, I've known for a while that there was *something* wrong. I could only speculate as to what that might be, of course; but now myriad clues are aligning, and it couldn't be more obvious.

"Why try and keep me out of this? Didn't you think I'd be able to piece it together? And are you seriously that pig-headed to ignore the reality of my father's last year? I mean, seriously? Alternative Chinese medicine?"

There was so much I could have said, and almost no time in which to say it.

The few garbled words I did manage must have looked like I was fumbling through a lie — which was almost certainly Alexa's impression, given the venom with which she launched her final assault.

"Come on, Jeff. You're not right in the head. No reasonable, rational man would do what you're doing. I'm sorry, but I can't do this. I can't sit back and watch you deteriorate like my father did."

And, with that, Alexa slammed her way out of the front door, suitcases in tow.

Goodbye, Jeff.

Newsletter 4:
Danny Hillis | 28ʳᵈ Nov, 2022

To our shareholders:

A part of me died when Alexa left, and that part of me became Santa Claus. To be sure, nothing changed at a cellular level. Anatomically, I was still the same Jeff.

The difference was mental.
My resolve changed.

In proving myself worthy in Alexa's eyes, I had to deliver on more than just a blanket. I needed the optimum Christmas gift; the gift of Christmas itself.

Throughout the next year, I brainstormed ideas that would turn my dream into a reality.

If my dream was to give everybody on Earth a gift, I needed vast warehouses — grottos, if you will — and lots of them.

As you know, warehouses don't come cheap. They belong to businesses, not people.

So, in a single car ride from New York City to Seattle, I settled on a business plan; one that established the necessary infrastructure for my transformation into Santa Claus.

The result of that cross-country drive was Amazon, and it remains my most productive commute to date. God knows how much better it could have been if I hadn't been driving at the same time.

*****

Since my plan to become Santa Claus could take three decades or more, I had to ask myself: was I planning on thirty-plus years of celibacy?

After quickly deciding that, no, I didn't have to live the life of a monk, I found myself a temporary partner, better known as, MacKenzie Scott Tuttle.

MacKenzie was, what I like to call, a marital pit-stop. By that, I mean: she served the purpose of satiating me until I was reunited with Alexa, the official destination of my journey.

***

In the early days of Amazon, we focused exclusively on books. Not only were they amongst the easiest things to deliver, they fast expanded our inventory, accustoming workers to process orders in the thousands; millions, even.

By 1998, I felt comfortable dipping my toes into screen. And, so, on April 27th, I bought the Internet Movie Database (best known by its acronym, IMDb).

This purchase marked an important change in Amazon's evolution. It cemented our image as more than just a bookshop, and it gave us a wealth of data for better understanding the tastes of our customers.

Data became the name of the game.

With enough of the right data, you can learn anything about anyone.

To be clear, I wasn't looking to make a Naughty of Nice list. I don't believe that there should be any conditions placed on your ability to enjoy Christmas.

What I wanted to know was exactly what gift each person wanted. In learning this, we had several engineers develop an algorithm that was designed to interpret our customer's data and, then, return to us their greatest desires.

In other words, the algorithm allowed us to read the minds of our customers.

For example, we punched Elon Musk's name into the algorithm and discovered that he loves diapers; not that I'm claiming he uses them, mind you.

That would be libelous.

***

We increased the scope of our data collection in 2014 with the release of Amazon's Alexa — our virtual assistant smart speaker. It allowed us to turn speech into data, which gave us an even greater insight into the psyches of our customers.

As you might imagine, I was keen to use the technology in better understanding the mind of Alexa.

My assistant, Andy Valentine, helped me with these insights. According to him, "The data told us that Alexa wanted a clock built inside a mountain."

At first, I didn't know what he meant.

But then Andy explained that her desire related to an idea presented by a scientist called Danny Hillis.

Hillis wanted to challenge man's idea of time.

Rather than use the traditional twelve or twenty-four-hour clock face, he proffered a new system; one that compartmentalized much larger units of time.

The design was based on a twelve-hour analogue clock. Where a normal clock would keep track of the passing seconds, the equivalent hand on Hillis' clock tracked each passing year.

His answer to the minute hand was one that moved an increment every century; and each passing hour was traded for a cuckoo that reared its head at the turn of every millennium.

***

Construction started in 2018.

We chose Texas as the best place for the clock; specifically, the Sierra Diablo mountain range — which was more than ideal for building a giant clock inside of it.

To date, I've pumped over $42 million into the operation.

***

Midway into the clock's construction, I became impatient. While my initial plan had been to gift Alexa the clock at Christmas upon the clock's completion, I convinced myself that I had already changed enough as a person to justify reaching out to her early.

It was still my intention to ensure that everyone on Earth received a present; but, until then, I planned on enjoying myself with the person I loved more than any other.

Simply put, life was too short to delay true romance. And, as far as I was concerned, I had completed enough of my transition into Santa Claus for Alexa to recognize me as a new man.

***

It didn't feel appropriate to break mine and Alexa's quarter-century silence over Facebook, so Andy Valentine, my assistant, reached out to her on my behalf.

Admittedly, he did so over Facebook.

The plan was for Alexa and I to meet in the main cavern of the hollowed-out mountain, stood in view of the cogs and mechanisms responsible for the clock's timekeeping (which, themselves, look like a contemporary art piece).

***

When the day in question arrived, I was pacing back and forth, taking swigs of water from a bottle whenever Andy presented it.

"Right, talk me through the plan again," I said. "Let's make sure we're on the same page."

"Okay," he agreed, consulting the notes attached to his clipboard. "Once she's here, I'll head upstairs to the control room and switch the lights off. Then, after a second or two of darkness, I'll illuminate the clock, leaving you to charm Alexa and explain the gift."

"And when will she get here?" I double-checked.

"I can't remember what time I said," he admitted. "But it's saved in your Google Calendar."

So, I opened my phone and loaded the voice-assistant. "Alexa, when is Alexa getting here?"

The screen briefly darkened, as if in contemplation, then lit back up with the verdict, "Alexa is already here."

Andy read the fear in my eyes and, so, assured me, "I think it's talking about itself."

Now, I'm not proud to admit this, but I threw my phone in exasperation. I watched it fly through the air, wincing as it splintered off a metal rod securing components of the clock in place.

"Jesus, Jeff," Andy said, looking up from his own phone at the *CLANG* of metal on metal. "What the hell are you doing?"
"Yeah," concurred a familiar voice behind me. *"What are you doing?"*

When I turned around, I was eye to eye with Alexa.

It was a jarring experience.
Twenty-five years is more than enough time to radically change a person. Though, that's not to say she looked like a different person entirely.
She was still undeniably Alexa, that much was sure. If I passed her in the street, I'd have known it was her. But I would have also kept my head down and prayed to God that she didn't notice me.
After all this time and effort, I'd managed the impossible and catfished myself.

She was hideous.

Her bloated, yet withering, face absorbed my attention, fully.

When she asked, again, "Why did you throw your phone like that?", the words went in and out of my ears without registering. I might never have twigged what she was talking about, if not for spying the shattered remains of my phone on the ground.

I made up an excuse as I went. "Ah, yeah... well, we started manufacturing indestructible phones. I thought that was one of them. But obviously not."

Alexa barely reacted, and not because my lie had failed. That same lie had a compelling effect on Andy, who, in a series of gradual footsteps away from us, asked, "Indestructible phones? Can I have one?"

Not wishing to appear callous, I lied again. "Absolutely. There's a load of them upstairs."

In reality, I was referring to the regular phones we kept in the control room; the ones intended as work phones for our construction workers.

Obviously, Andy didn't need to know that these phones weren't indestructible. I would come clean about the truth once Alexa left.

"Take one, if you like," I told Andy.
He nodded his appreciation. "Thanks. I will."

With that, Andy's footsteps faded.
Then it was back to just Alexa and I, together again like the old days.

Clearly, though, *things were different.*
I felt lonely in her company, for a start.
Her eyes were still that same striking green... only colder and more calculating; reptilian, even.

All of this woke me up to how stupid I'd been.

I had spent nearly $50 million hollowing out one of my perfectly good mountains.

Suffice it to say, I was no longer planning on gifting Hillis' clock to Alexa.

Of course, there could be no way of letting Andy know about my change of heart now. He was going to go ahead with our original plan, and I had to conceive of some way around it.

***

"I've got a bone to pick with you," Alexa started.

My stomach tightened. "Yeah?"

"Did you really have to sully my name with your awful virtual assistant thing?"

I was on the verge of answering when the lights clunked off.

The darkness was abrupt enough to daze me, and I'd been expecting it; so, it was hardly surprising that Alexa drew closer and whimpered, "What happened?"

If I was still following the plan, this would have been when I declared my love for her.

Since that no longer felt like an option, I told her, "There's been a power cut."

No sooner had I made my diagnosis, the lights from the clock burst on behind me. They created a warm glow, which stretched mine and Alexa's shadows out across the jagged wall in front of us.

Her focus was on the light when she made her observation, "Doesn't look like a power cut."

She was right.

A power cut didn't make sense.

But I muttered something about solar panels and that was enough to change the subject.

"What's going on, Jeff?" she asked, finally. "Why did you invite me here?"

It was a bloody good question, and I wished I had a better answer.

In the end, I could think of no way out but to deny ever having invited her. "I don't know what happened," I said. "There must have been a mix-up."

Alexa did a good job of keeping her cool, all things considered. She pulled her phone from her purse and asked, "Do you have the time? My phone's dead."

Reaching for my own device, I grazed an empty pocket.

"Ah," I remembered, drawn to the remnants of metal, glass, and plastic strewn across the floor. "Mine's dead too."

She stopped herself mid-eyeroll and looked around the cavern. "Well, don't you have a clock here? I've got a taxi coming at half past."

The giant clock behind me didn't escape my attention. But I kept this fact to myself. I didn't want Alexa to see it, lest she desire it like our algorithm said she would.

My only recourse was to defer my answer to Andy. That's why, I hollered his name, praying that he would come and save me.

***

Andy returned about half a minute later, a smile on his face.

Alexa asked him, "Do you have the time?", and he doubled over laughing.

"What's so funny?" she asked.

"Well, you've been gifted this huge clock," he said, grinning at the thought. "And here you are asking for the time."

I knew we had a problem when Alexa asked him what clock he was talking about.

I tried to come between them, but Andy caught my eye. "What's going on?" he said. "Didn't you ask her yet?"

"Ask me what?" Alexa cut in.

Andy's head sunk forward in embarrassment. "Mr. Bezos, I'm sorry. Did I ruin the surprise?"

Obviously, Alexa was curious what Andy meant by 'surprise'. Thankfully, I didn't have to come out with that information.

Because Andy told her immediately.

***

"Let's get things straight," Alexa said, massaging her eyelids. "You built a $43 million clock inside a mountain... for me?"

I couldn't muster the words to explain myself. I simply let my tired head fall forward into something that might be interpreted as a nod.

"How on earth could you think I'd actually like this?" she scolded.

Once again, no words came.

Fortunately for me, Andy was just as invested as I was. "With all due respect, Alexa, an algorithm said that this would be the perfect gift for you."

"Well, check it again," she rebutted. "There's no way I'd ever need a giant clock inside a mountain."

It already felt like more of Andy's fight than mine. So, I sat back and watched as he asked, "What if you're in a mountain and your phone runs out of battery? Like your present situation?"

Not wishing to give him the satisfaction of an agreement, she brought her hands to her hips and sighed, "Just tell me what time it is."

Apparently, she didn't like hearing we were only eighteen years past the first century, and not just because she didn't what know that meant.
After learning that the clock operated over larger units of time, she told me she wouldn't be alive in one hundred years, let alone ten thousand.

"You're both crazy," she shouted, backing out of the cavern, leaving nothing but her echo.

Andy and I were muzzled by the situation.

We stood in silence, until maybe a minute after Alexa was gone, when Andy reflected aloud, "One day, I hope I get to meet my soulmate too."

Then he apologized, "Sorry it didn't work out, Jeff."

I brushed it off and told him it didn't matter.

"But I would like to know what went wrong with the algorithm's prediction," I noted. "We can't afford any more mistakes like that. Understood?"

He nodded so passionately, he looked on the brink of saluting. "Absolutely," he agreed. "I'll look into it at once."

***

Andy returned around ten minutes later.

He loitered for a second before speaking.

"Remember when we tried to read Elon Musk's mind by having the algorithm guess his most desired product?"

How could I forget?

"Well," Andy continued, clutching the clipboard to his chest. "Looks like I didn't clear the search bar. It was Elon who wanted Hillis' clock inside a mountain."

To our shareholders:

Knowing that Alexa, now, exceeded the maximum age to qualify as my muse, the next six months were the most directionless of my life.

All of a sudden, it felt like everything had been for nothing. What's the point in owning a multi-billion-dollar e-commerce conglomerate, if you've got no intention of leveraging it to become Santa Claus?

I had a full-blown identity crisis.

To be robbed of motivation is to be robbed of your essence; a lobotomy of sorts. Forbes called me the richest man in the world, yet I didn't know who I was. And, apparently, I wasn't the only one. Elon Musk didn't know who I was either.

When posed with my name in a BBC interview, Elon snidely remarked, "Jeff *who*?"

It was surely facetious. Elon and I had met several times before, so it seemed unlikely that he hadn't learned my name.

The only reasonable conclusion, then, was that his retort was steeped in contempt for my life and work.

Jeff who?

Jeff Bezos: Santa Claus, that's *who*.

In a flash, it was obvious.

I wasn't becoming Santa Claus for Alexa; I was becoming Santa Claus for everybody else.

It was time to show the public what a *real* man of the people looked like. A real man of the people didn't make his money selling expensive cars. A real man of the people made his money in pursuit of Christmas, and he shared his wealth amongst everybody.

Every single person would get a gift from me.

That's right. Even *you.*

Hell, *even Elon.*

Although, to be honest, I was going to have a little fun with Elon's gift.

The plan was to give him what our algorithm said he wanted more than anything in the world: Danny Hillis' clock inside a mountain.

When the magnitude of the gift had sunk in, I was going to surprise him further with a little firework show.

I'd detonate the Sierra Diablo mountain range and take that damn clock with it. An expensive mistake, all told, but at least I'd close that chapter with a bang.

***

Since I no longer planned to tie the knot with Alexa, it was finally time to start living my life. And, so, in 2019, after twenty-six years at the same pitstop, MacKenzie and I filed for divorce.

It wasn't long before I fell in love with someone new; media personality, Lauren Sánchez.

48

Safe to say, I was smitten immediately. The thought that I ever spent time chasing Alexa started to feel like a hilarious joke.

But the hardest thing about having a beautiful girlfriend is keeping them interested. Scores of men will compete for your girlfriend's attention.
If you can't keep them satisfied, their eyes are bound to wander.

***

I was ready to employ every trick in the book, if it meant keeping Lauren by my side. And this is how I came to approach Andy Valentine again.
"Andy," I said. "I need your help. Tell me: which gift would Lauren appreciate more than any other?"

At my request, Andy withdrew his phone and loaded the results of our algorithm.
"It says here that her optimal gift would be a series of *The Lord of the Rings*, with the narrative set in the Second Age of Middle-earth."

"Hang on," I stalled. "You said, a *series*? Wouldn't she be happy with a Blu-ray boxset of Peter Jackson's trilogy?"

But Andy grimaced and shook his head.
And that's how I came to greenlight Amazon's *The Lord of the Rings: The Rings of Power*, which set me back $462 million — easily triple that of Peter Jackson's Blu-ray boxset.

It was important to me that I get the series right, and even more important that it remain a surprise.

So, I kept my mouth shut and didn't mention a thing to Lauren until the night of the premiere.

***

The premiere took place on August 30th 2022 at Cineworld in Leicester Square, London.

Lauren and I flew to England a few days earlier, with me explaining the trip as a simple romantic getaway.

"Surprise," I said, as a limousine pulled up in front of our hotel.

"What's going on?" Lauren asked.

"I've been working on a series set in *The Lord of the Rings* universe," I told her. "It's a present from me to you. And the premiere's tonight."

I couldn't help but feel that Lauren seemed rather unenthusiastic during our drive in the limousine, so I attempted to reenergize proceedings.

"It's nice to finally talk to you about *The Lord of the Rings*," I said. "I've held off from talking about it until now because I wanted this evening to remain a surprise. So, tell me, because I'm dying to know, how did you first get into Tolkien?"

Lauren sipped her flute of champagne before giving an answer. "I know the name," she said. "But I don't know much about him."

***

Upon arriving at Leicester Square, I excused myself and made a phone call to Andy Valentine.

"Andy," I said, in a tone he instantly recognized as serious. "Are you sure that Lauren wanted a series made in *The Lord of the Rings* universe?"

There was silence as he searched for his answer.
Then came the exhalation, "Ah, shit."

When I asked him what was wrong, Andy told me, "You were right. She didn't want a series. She wanted a film."

But that still didn't sit right with me.
If I didn't know any better, I'd say Lauren didn't want anything *Lord of the Rings* related at all.

It was another several seconds before I heard, "Ah, shit," again, this time, even louder.
Eventually, Andy admitted, "I forgot to clear the search bar again. *Lord of the Rings* was for Elon."

I wasn't in the quietest of environments, and I didn't feel like drawing attention to myself. So, while I was annoyed, Andy caught nothing of it.

"I thought Elon wanted the clock," I said.
"He does," Andy agreed. "The clock was his second choice."

Again, I held my tongue.
"Let me get this straight," I said. "Are you saying that I've wasted half a billion dollars on the first and second item of Elon's Christmas list?"

He wavered before confessing, "I'm afraid not."
What came next should have been obvious. Nevertheless, Andy's words hit me like a ton of bricks.

"The Lord of the Rings was his third choice."

Anger bubbled in my stomach.
It took me a second to stifle it. *"Third choice?"*

Andy was too ashamed for words. "Mm-hmm."

Obviously, I couldn't help but ask him, "What the hell was his first choice?"

At that, he smacked his lips together and said, "His first choice was diapers."

***

My pre-premiere anxiety was through the roof. I only made it through the evening by make-believing that Lauren was a bona fide Tolkienite.

To cut a long story short, it seemed that Lauren genuinely enjoyed herself. Sure, she no doubt exaggerated her interest out of politeness, but she also seemed genuinely captivated by the story.

Lauren's opinion aside, the critics were suitably impressed. And the first two episodes pulled twenty-five million views in twenty-four hours.
From where I was standing, it looked like we had a hit.

And then Elon Musk chimed in with his verdict.

Ordinarily, I wouldn't have cared for what he thought. But since the series had, in fact, been made for him specifically, I felt a duty to lend him my ears.

Hearing Elon claim, "Tolkien is turning in his grave," was a real punch to the gut, and not just because I didn't know Tolkien was dead.

Our algorithm was designed to unite people with the products they love, and, so, Elon's disdain for the series suggested we'd either misprogrammed the algorithm, or failed to make the show as good as it was supposed to be.

Back in Seattle, I relayed my concerns to Andy who assured me the algorithm was fine.

According to him, it was *The Lord of the Rings* series that was lacking.

In any case, I told Andy, "Make a spreadsheet with three columns. The first should list every single person on Earth; the second, their address; and the third, the gift they most desire, as determined by the algorithm. Keep it saved on your phone, offline, and we won't have any more mix-ups."

***

What I requested of Andy was no small feat, yet he accepted the job as he would a request to make coffee.

In all fairness, the spreadsheet's three columns made for easy work. It was the eight billion rows that took him slightly longer.

He coded a program that scraped the name and address of every person with a digital profile. That information was then deposited into the first and second column of the spreadsheet.

The spreadsheet's third column could only be populated when the person in question had an Amazon account with purchasing history. Individuals lacking this information were assigned gifts at random.

***

All told, it was an excruciating effort.

Andy didn't finish it until a week before Christmas.

By then, everything was ready for the big day.
Fulfilment centers around the globe were stocked to the brim with inventory, and I bought myself a red suit, fit with the red, jangly hat.
I even had a red sleigh custom-built.

I was one click away from importing nine reindeer from Siberia, when Andy told me that the bastards can't fly.
Thankfully, I was informed of my error before it came to wasting money. I put an order in for nine of the biggest birds I could think of instead.
And, just like that, a flock of ostriches were on their way.

For your information, the sleigh and the suit were mere decoration. I wasn't planning on dressing up and delivering the presents myself.
My trusted network of drivers would see to that.
All I planned on doing was flying my sleigh as a gimmick — delivering Christmas cheer to anyone ready to receive it.

The only part of the plan I doubted was the strength of the explosives reserved for blasting the Sierra Diablo into smithereens.

***

Andy suggested we schedule a test explosion to calm my nerves. So, on the afternoon of December 18th, we took several sticks of dynamite to a dry, but otherwise unoccupied, stretch of land not far from the site of the clock.

Since it's not every day that you get to play with dynamite, I made an event of it. I still owned several items left over from my relationship with Alexa, and turning them into an effigy of her seemed like a good idea.

"It's symbolic," I told Andy, draping an old pair of jeans over a bag she'd once owned, emulating hair on a head. "It marks the end of the Alexa era."

Andy stood with his arms behind his back, every bit the spare part.

"Come on, man," I said, slapping his back. "It's supposed to be cathartic. Don't you have anything you want to blow up?"

"Oh, no, no," Andy replied. "This is your thing."

"For the love of God," I said. "Always follow-through with the things I tell you to do. We're not blowing this up until you add something to the pile."

***

Five minutes later, I was stood a hundred or so yards away in a safe zone, decked out in protective goggles.
Andy was back with the dynamite, lighting the wick of each stick. As soon as he had them lit, he sprinted in the direction of where I was standing.

His hands were up around his head when he arrived by my side. For a second, all I could hear was his breathing. But then an almighty BANG drowned everything out, leaving a ringing of the ears in its wake.

***

In the aftermath of the blast, as dust and debris descended to the ground, a hilarious idea came to me. "You know what would make this better?"

A smile formed on my lips, but I held off from laughing. "We should pack the mountain with diapers. Not only will it look hysterical when they start raining down, we'll have destroyed the two things that Elon loves most: the clock and diapers."

Now, when you've got as much money as me, you have to be mindful of yes-men. They'll sidle up to you; tell you what you want to hear; and, generally, act the air pump to your ego.

That's why it's always relieving to come up with an idea as good as stuffing a mountain full of diapers. There's no second-guessing yourself when it comes to an idea that good.

And, so, when Andy told me, "Great idea, boss," I knew he wasn't lying. Because, let's face it, *it was a great idea.*

"Add that detail to the spreadsheet," I told him. "Next to Elon's name, write down the clock *and diapers.*"

At that, Andy nodded.

And then he began turning, and walking, in the direction of the explosion.

"Wait," I said, pulling at his shoulder. "Where are you going?"

"I need my phone for the spreadsheet," he said.

I followed his finger to the site of the detonation. "Why the hell was it over there? I asked.

"You told me to empty my pockets."

"So, you blew up your phone?" I snapped.

"Don't worry," he said, tapping his nose and winking. "It's indestructible."

To our shareholders:

As you probably guessed, Andy's phone *wasn't* indestructible; and, because he had saved the spreadsheet *offline*, this meant, the list of everybody and their most desired present had been blasted into non-existence.

But that wasn't my only problem.

On December 21st, I opened my front door to a delivery driver, fitted in cargo shorts and a boonie hat. "Delivery for Mr. Bezos," he said.

I stared at the crates spread across my lawn.
With so little time left until Christmas, I couldn't help but sound put out. "Jesus, what the hell is this?"

He checked the piece of paper in his hand.
"You ordered nine ostriches, right?"

Suddenly, it all made sense. "Oh, yes. Great."

"So, where do you want them?" he asked.

I pointed to the fence that lined the perimeter of my garden, singling out the bit farthest from the road. "Leave them over there," I instructed. "But tie them up. The last thing I need is them flying away."

In response to that, the delivery man laughed, and that's why I pressured him, "What's funny?"

"Ostriches are flightless," he said.

It was an annoying error, but, in this game, you roll with the punches. And, anyway, it wasn't long before we found a solution.

The solution came while Andy and I were working on the spreadsheet.

In doing so, the algorithm determined that nine people — all within a reasonable vicinity of my house — wanted an ostrich more than any other gift.

Sometimes, these problems sort themselves out.

***

One problem that wasn't going to sort itself out was the problem of my sleigh achieving flight.

Thankfully, Amazon had long since begun work in drone technology. By this time, our devices were sufficiently advanced.

A collaboration between my best engineers from Amazon and Blue Origin produced a blueprint for the perfect configuration of drones. This configuration, they said, would take my sleigh to the skies.

All I had to do was hold the reins, which were carefully tethered to each of the electronic aircrafts.

The engineers would pilot me from Amazon HQ.

***

With a couple of hours to spare, Andy completed the spreadsheet for the second time. The information gathered in each of the cells was then relayed to a program, and that program got to work ordering each person's ideal gift.

When I was certain that every order had gone through, and I was satisfied that my fulfilment centers had receipt of the orders, I got myself ready for a night in my sleigh, delivering Christmas cheer and ostriches.

After dressing in my red suit and hat, I bundled all nine ostriches into the back of the sleigh.

They hissed, spat, and cawed when I climbed onto the seat in front of them, pecking my head as the drones whirred to life.

The drones raced away at a terrific speed, hauling me, the sleigh, and the ostriches, with it.

It was a bumpy ride at first, but the flying robots soon gained enough height for us to glide effortlessly over the ground.

Before long, we were soaring over Texas and I was feeling exhilarated. From up here, the people looked like ants, and the ants looked like baby ants.

***

The engineers back at Amazon HQ devised a route that took me from house to house, visiting all nine individuals that most wanted ostriches.

We landed on the first roof around midnight.

The streets were quiet, save for the occasional car driving by, apparently unaware of my presence above them.

***

In many ways, I was far better suited to being Santa Claus than Santa Claus himself.

My slim, yet muscular, physique made easy work of the chimneys. I could traverse up and down the passageways, no problem.

The ostriches had a harder time.

I'd hoist them into the mouth of the chimney and let gravity do its work.
They'd cluck, cluck, cluck on the way down, breaking their fall in a mattress of feathers.

It wasn't until my delivery attempt at the second house that an ostrich became stuck midway down the shaft. I had to use my weight to dislodge the thing.
I jumped up and down on the bird's head until we both broke free and tumbled into the fireplace.

"Who the hell is that?"

The voice belonged to a woman, though, the age was hard to determine.

A racket of footsteps followed.

Within seconds, the living room door whipped open and a woman wearing a dressing gown came barging in. She grabbed a lampshade from the table next to her, ripping its cord from the socket.

"Ah! Ah!" she screamed, pummeling my face with the light. "Get the fuck out of my house!"

The ostrich didn't appreciate the commotion.
It rose on spindly legs and beelined for the sofa, trampling shit and dirt into their rug. Then commenced its defacement of the sofa, which it tore with its beak and spat into a flurry of feathers.

The range of sounds it produced while doing so was extraordinary. As you'd expect, there was the usual squawking and hissing; but I never expected to hear it *ROAR*.

With distractions such as these, I didn't register the young girl enter the room.

"Mommy!" she shouted, pulling the back of her mother's dressing gown. "Stop it! You're hurting Santa!"

I was too busy avoiding concussion to find the situation funny. But whenever I think back to the little girl and imagine what must have been going through her mind, I can't help but laugh.

From her perspective, Santa was *supposed* to be in her living room. It was Christmas Eve night, after all, and that was the time he delivered presents.

And, of course, she had good reason to believe this.

Her mother and father corroborated the lie her whole life. They no doubt encouraged her to leave a serving of milk and cookies in anticipation of his arrival.

It's hardly surprising, then, that the little girl cried so much at the sight of her mother beating the shit out of the man she believed to be Santa Claus.

***

In response to her daughter's protestations, the mother pushed her backwards and said, "Go to your room and don't come out until I say it's safe!"

She didn't wait to see if her instructions were heeded. Her hands and the lampshade recommenced their assault, causing me to shield myself in the fetal position.

"Mommy! Stop!" the little girl squealed, pulling the same spot on her dressing gown.

By this point, the mother was in a blind fury. To her, this was life-or-death and her maternal instincts kicked in.
She swatted away her daughter with her free hand and used the other to paint my face with bruises.

I was well on my way to becoming black and blue when a man entered the room.

"Daddy!" the girl shouted, scampering to him. "Mommy won't stop hitting Santa!"

Somehow, this was enough to stop the punches.

But I was more than a little disoriented.

My sense of everybody's position in the room came from what I could sense through my ear, which was mushed against the floorboards.
Erratic scratching told me that the ostrich had tired of the sofa and was back on the move.
Neither the man, woman, or girl, made a sound.

That whole time, I didn't dare open my eyes.

I was bracing myself for another beating.

***

At least ten seconds passed before the next footfall. It belonged to the father, that much was sure.

Each weighty step brought him closer to me, until he stood so near, I could hear him breathing.

The storm of his breath thundered so close, the air from his nostrils warmed my scalp. As it did, the woman agonized behind him, "Be careful, Darren."

Grunting, Darren forced both hands under my armpit. "Oh my God," he said, flipping me onto my back.

"What's wrong?" his partner cut in.

"Is Santa going to be okay?" the little girl added.

I watched the woman place a protective arm around the girl, pulling her closer. "Olivia, that's not Santa. A very naughty man broke into our house."

But Olivia tore free of her mother's grasp and ran toward her father and I.

"Daddy, tell her!" she pleaded, clutching his pajama pants and shaking his legs.

Darren had seen enough to dismiss me as a threat. "For God's sake, Brenda," he said, standing up straight. "Don't you know who this is? You've just given the richest man in the world brain damage. Do you think he'll let us forget that?"

To be fair to Brenda, she was more than sorry. Her eyes grew maniacally large, and she came between myself and Darren.

"I'm so sorry," she said, squeezing my shoulder. "Mr. Musk, I hope you can forgive me."

I felt compelled to correct her, but Darren chimed in on my behalf. "Brenda, it's Jeff Bezos."

"It's not!" shouted Olivia. "It's Santa Claus!"

***

Darren and Brenda insisted that I stay, so it was another forty minutes before I left the premises.

They placed me on the sofa and pulled my feet onto an ottoman. With me lay back, they cleansed the scars and bruising on my face.

We shared a couple of brandies too.

For me, it numbed the pain. For them, it was an excuse to drink.

All in all, it was a costly hour. Not only had my body incurred significant damage, it was all for nothing.

Since neither the man or woman wanted the ostrich, they helped me return it to my sleigh on top of their roof.

Then, after thanking each other for not pressing charges, I flapped at my reins and took to the skies, soaring over Texan suburbia.

***

I saved time at the third house by climbing through a window, opening it wide enough for an ostrich to slip inside.

I then made up for my failed delivery at Darren and Brenda's house by coaxing *two* ostriches into the building.

***

The ostriches hissed and squawked en route to the fourth house.

As I was about to discover, their ruckus was in response to something I hadn't yet seen.

Before I knew it, a great hum rose up behind us. It felt like the King Kong of wasps was in pursuit.

A flashing red and blue light got me to turn around. When I did, I was eye to eye with a police helicopter.

Fortunately, the engineers back at Amazon HQ saw the helicopter too.

At once, the drones began their descent.

We pulled over onto the side of a road, and the helicopter followed suit behind.

***

The propellors whirred to a halt.

Two officers in uniform stepped out of the craft, jumping from the foot of the door to the asphalt.

They eyed the ostriches with caution.

When they arrived next to me, their hands were on their weapons.

"Do you have any idea why we pulled you over?"

In all honesty, I had no idea.
But I was curious.

I didn't know which specific laws I'd broken, but I was willing to believe that I was in violation of some of them.

"Your taillights are out," the tallest officer said.

"That's it?" I asked.

"Wait a second," the other interjected, sniffing at the air. "Have you been drinking?"

Damn. I didn't think about that.
Did a couple of brandies count?
It was Christmas, after all...

"I'm sorry, officers," I said. "I've had one or two drinks."

The smaller officer nudged his colleague. "Grab the breathalyzer."

***

Talk about a Christmas miracle.
I blew just below the legal limit.

"Sorry to have bothered you," they apologized, turning back toward their helicopter.

They were several steps away when the walkie talkies on their belts began broadcasting, "We've got a report of a breaking and entering. Suspect got away in a red sleigh, wearing a red suit; and he left behind two ostriches."

That's when they turned back to me, with occasional side glances at the sleigh and my six remaining ostriches.
"I don't suppose you know anything about this?"

Obviously, I knew everything about it.
And that's how I ended up at the police department.

To our shareholders:

My home for the night was a temporary holding cell.

Bail was set at five thousand dollars, and they gave me one phone call in which to secure it.

I could not leave my cell unsupervised, so an officer escorted me to the landline. He idled over my shoulder as I dialed for the only man who could help.

Andy picked up before it had a chance to ring.

He began speaking immediately, the concern thick in his voice. "Jeff?"

I couldn't help but smile.

I was on a payphone with no caller ID, yet he instantly sensed my presence.

But, apparently, I was on a time limit, and the accompanying officer didn't want me to forget it.

He prodded my back and made circular motions with his hand, as if to say, "Hurry up."

So, I cut to the chase and told Andy what I needed. And that was five thousand dollars, as quickly as possible.

"Of course, Mr. Bezos," is what I had expected to hear, but he told me, "You don't have five thousand dollars; you spent everything," instead.

With the clock-watching officer so close behind me, I jumped to the most obvious solution first.

"Sell my share of the company."

Silence is one of life's great tattlers.
In this instance, it was loud and clear: selling my Amazon stock was out of the question.

When Andy finally spoke, he said, "I can see why you'd suggest that. It was my first idea as well."

"What changed your mind?" I asked.

"Well, we tried it and it didn't work."

***

Yes, that's right. He already sold all of my stock. But even that wasn't enough to cover eight billion presents.

According to Andy, I needed to change my priorities if I was to continue living a fulfilled life.
"You don't need money to be happy," he told me. "Some of the happiest people I know have nothing. The problem is, you need two-hundred billion dollars to have nothing; that's how much you're overdrawn."

Shortly thereafter, I was made to end the call.
After that, despondency disabled me.

Lumbering back to the cell, my shoes scuffed the ground so much that the officer snapped, "Lift your feet up, Joe."
His use of the name Joe, instead of Jeff, barely registered. If he wanted to call me Joe, so be it. I had al-ready lost everything; why not my identity as well?

***

The same officer guarded my cell for the remainder of that day.

He sat in a plastic chair, angled partly at me; partly at an outdated box of a television.

I couldn't see the screen from my cell.

All I got was the tinny noise from its, less-than-stellar, speaker system.

He clicked between channels, periodically — from the schmoozy speak of advertisements, to the serious talk of the news.

It was during one of these stints on the news that my ears picked up, "Is it a bird? Is it a plane? Or is it a sleigh, an ostrich, and the world's richest man?"

The officer noted my piqued interest.

He turned to me and said, "What do you know? Looks like Elon Musk is just as stupid as you."

With that, he rose, pressed off the television's power button, and then he stretched back upon his chair, yawning.

I felt like an idiot for speaking, but I had to clear things up. "I think they're talking about me."

The officer laughed so hard, he started coughing. "Are you deaf as well as poor? How could you be the world's richest man? You can't afford bail."

"Please," I begged, edging closer to the bars. "I *was* the world's richest man."

"That's what they all say," he tutted.

***

Most of the officers agreed that Elon Musk was Santa Claus. According to them, a decent percentage of the general population believed the same.

In other words, my transformation was a failure.

I hadn't recaptured Alexa's heart, and Elon dominated the zeitgeist more than ever. Worse than that, it was *my hard work* that more securely fastened him to the upholstery of culture.

If only there was a way of flipping the tide and blasting his name into obscurity...

***

Of course, not everybody believed Elon Musk was Santa Claus.

At one point, two police officers walked past my cell, with the first saying to the other, "It wasn't Elon. I heard it was Jeff Bezos."

"Jeff *who*?"

Hearing those words was a call to action.

I couldn't help myself.

I stood up and yelled, "He said, Jeff Bezos."

The commotion caused the second officer to stop in his tracks. "And who the hell are you?"

It would seem that "Jeff Bezos" wasn't the answer he was looking for. He couldn't accept that I played any part in the Santa Claus hijinks.

"This has Elon written all over it," he said.

"Look," I bargained. "I can prove that Elon had nothing to do with it. You see, I have one final present to deliver, and Elon is the recipient of it. It's currently wrapped up in the Sierra Diablo mountain range."

Both of the officers laughed. "Let me get this straight, you want us to take you to a mountain? What's in it for us?"

I almost promised them an ostrich each, forgetting that the birds had been confiscated by the state of Texas.

"Erm, well," I stalled. "There's a bunch of phones in the mountain's control room. You can take as many of them as you want."

They shrugged. "We've already got phones."

"Yes," I said. "But are yours indestructible?"

***

Following several back-and-forth exchanges, the police reunited me with my phone.

At the first available moment, I brought Andy up to speed, getting him to find Elon's number so that we could arrange a meeting.

"You'll find us at the Sierra Diablo mountain range," I told Elon. "Trust me. You'll erupt with excitement."

***

With Elon on board, there was no shortage of officers wishing to accompany us. In the end, a rock paper scissors tournament decided who came.

Andy met us at the entrance to the mountain.
He shook hands with the officers one by one, then he pulled me to one side and whispered, "What are they doing here?"

"They want to meet Elon," I told him.

And that's when I discovered there had been a near-fatal misunderstanding in our communication.

"Won't the police be suspicious if they see us blow up Elon?"

***

Just so we're clear, Andy got the wrong end of the stick. Sure, I may have wanted to blow up the clock, thereby destroying part of the mountain, but I had no intention of including Elon in the mayhem.
My plan had been for Elon to fall in love with the clock, then, when he was a safe distance away from it, blow it to rubble right in front of his stupid face.

But there wasn't time for any of that right now because the policemen were asking, "Where's our indestructible phones?"

***

On our way to retrieve the phones, Andy blocked my path. His voice was shaky, borderline stuttering. "Where... where are you going?"

"I promised the officers a phone," I said.

His bulbous eyes betrayed the fact that something was troubling him. He leant into my ear and told me, "Don't take them in there."

My eyes were stern. My lips were pursed.
Andy knew I needed to know why.

By now, he was shaking his head. "Just don't take them in there."

"All right," I decided. "I'll get the phones myself." Then, after a side-glance at the officers, I told Andy, "You keep them busy."

Without missing a beat, he made his way over to the policemen. He turned their attentions to the surrounding landscape, and lectured them on the area's history.

Meanwhile, I went into autopilot.

I unlocked the door, and disengaged the burglar alarm. I then proceeded into the main cavern, targeting the control room.

The cavern was dimly lit, though, not as dark as usual. There was a whiteness on the floor that gave a dull illumination.

Hang on a minute... is that snow?

***

In grazing my hand through the white stuff, I realized, it wasn't snow at all.

It didn't numb my hand with cold, and it became more of an off-white under the harshness of the cavern's main lights.

Upon closer inspection, it was obvious.

It turns out, Andy had covered the cavern in diapers. Hundreds of thousands (possibly, millions) of them.

***

In pursuit of the control room, I traversed the assault course of diapers.

After grabbing the phones, I made my way back outside. In doing so, I discovered that everybody had arranged themselves into a semi-circle.

It won't surprise you to hear that Elon Musk was at the head of the makeshift amphitheater, holding court. He cradled a baby in each arm, with another seven or eight kids dotted around him.

It was the weakest security team I'd ever seen.

***

Elon stopped what he was saying as soon as he saw me, which caused everybody else to follow his gaze.

He nodded my way and I nodded back, walking to him with my hand held out for him to shake.

God knows why I went to shake his hand; he was carrying too many babies for that.

He rolled his eyes. "What's this gift you want to give me?"

"Well," I said, ready to commence a rehearsed speech dedicated to the clock...

But then Elon's nostrils flared.

He sniffed the baby in his left arm and only just avoided retching. "For God's sake."

I didn't need to ask him what had happened. I could smell the problem from where I was standing.

So, I told him, "If you need to use our facilities, let me know."

Elon offloaded the baby in his right arm to his eldest child; then he repositioned the baby in soiled underwear, so as to make sure that it didn't touch his clothing.

"It's a long shot," he said. "But do you have any diapers inside?"

***

Everybody followed in a single file, except for Andy. He raced to the front and asked, "What's going on?"

"Elon needs a diaper," I said.

I was so focused on this mission that Andy's discomfort didn't register.

I slipped ahead of him again and led the way to the main section of the cavern.

"What's this?" Elon staggered, swiveling around to face the white surroundings.

The officers were behind him a second or two later, echoing variations of the same question.

All eyes were on Elon as he squatted to touch the white. "You filled the mountain with diapers?"

My attention went to Andy, who was stood with his arms behind his back, focusing on the ground.

"Erm," I began, now looking from Andy to Elon. "That's right. I filled the mountain with diapers."

By now, everybody was looking at me.

I was about to intellectualize things by talking about the algorithm. I was going to explain what our algorithm had revealed about Elon's material preferences, and then make a show of presenting him with the gifts.

But before I could, he plucked a diaper from the ground and said, "Well, I'll take one of these, if you don't mind?"

In the corner of my eye, Andy became more and more restless. It was like he couldn't choose between intervening or getting the hell out of there.

Then, all of a sudden, the cause of his agitation was obvious. Elon, who had walked a couple of paces in the direction of the bathroom, exclaimed, "Ugh!", and threw the diaper to the floor.

"What the fuck was that?" he recoiled, almost dropping the baby.

Once again, all eyes were on Elon.

He held his fingers under his nose and grimaced, "Jeff, was there shit in that diaper?"

I liked Andy too much to draw attention his way, but there were certainly some questions I would have loved to ask:

"*Was* there really shit in that diaper?"
If so, "*Why* was there shit in that diaper?"
And, "Did you fill *all* of the diapers with shit?"
If yes, "*How* did you fill all of them with shit?"

It seems, these same questions were on every-body's mind, as evidenced by their attempts to answer them.

One of the officers, for instance, crouched down and sniffed the diaper at his feet. "There's shit in this one."

Shortly thereafter, another officer lowered his nose to the diapers he found himself stood upon.

"Yeah," he agreed. "There's shit in these as well."

Andy became so self-conscious that it was even obvious in my periphery. From his perspective, what followed was a forgone conclusion: everybody was about to learn that he had — somehow — filled all of the cav-ern's diapers with excrement.

***

When one of the officers trudged toward me and asked, "Why do all of these diapers have poo in them?", I couldn't bring myself to point to Andy.

"Well," I said. "That's because I took a shit in all of them."

You can only imagine the look on their faces.

No one looked capable of talking any time soon, save for Andy who mouthed the words, "Thank you."

***

Before I had chance to break the silence, an officer scooped my hands behind my back and slipped my wrists into handcuffs. "I think we've seen enough."

"Wait a minute," I resisted. "Why are you cuffing me? I proved that I was Santa Claus, didn't I?"

"Well, not really," the same officer said. "But that's beside the point. You weren't guilty of *not* being Santa Claus; you were guilty of breaking and entering. And, let's face it, shitting into hundreds of thousands of diapers may as well be a crime."

Prison felt like a grim resolution, yet I felt inconvenienced more than sad. "In that case, why the hell did you bother bringing me here?"

None of the officers were quick to speak.
Eventually, the youngest of the group made the admission, "We wanted to meet Mr. Musk."

Elon pouted at the news, as if their fascination for him depended on how he looked.
Seconds later, two hands fastened under each of my armpits, and I found myself dragged from the cavern.
According to Elon's children, this ranked amongst the funniest things they'd ever seen. They whooped and hollered for as long as it took the officers to haul me outside.

At the last minute, I shouted to Elon, "Merry Christmas! The diapers; the clock; it's all for you!"

"Give it to somebody else," he yelled back. "It's a load of shite. All I'd do is blow it up."

To our shareholders:

In many ways, I achieved what I set out to do: I gave all of my money away; gifted everybody on Earth Christmas presents; and, in the process, created one of the world's most successful companies.

As with all efforts, there were a couple of unintended consequences. I hadn't expected to bankrupt myself in making my dreams a reality, and I could have done without a twenty-year jail sentence for identity theft, trespassing, breaking and entering, unauthorized use of a vehicle, and cruelty to animals.

On account of my notoriety, I've been homed in a private cell. At first, this seemed to me like a privilege, but the degenerative effects of loneliness soon reared its ugly head.

Thankfully, life before my incarceration had been so rich and fulfilling that I was able to alleviate the pain of my present situation with the company of memories.

I spent whole days in bed, reliving earlier episodes of my life, and played out imaginary conversations between myself and those that I loved and valued most.

***

It was a morning like any other.

With no reason to rise, I dozed in and out of sleep. That was, until a patter of footsteps clicked down the corridor, stopping at my cell.

It was breakfast time.

The door creaked open, revealing one of the guards. They called around this time every morning, with a tray of sliced bread and coffee in hand.

However, today, the guard came with a message. "You've got a visitor," he said, turning back in the direction of more footsteps.

I felt under siege.

My only means of defense was to prop myself up against the support of the bed and ask, "Who is it?"

"She said her name was Alexa."

The tip-tapping of feet drew closer.

My palms began to sweat.

"Please," I said, reduced to a whisper. "I'm not accepting visitors right now."

The guard's lips scrunched in confusion, clearly unaccustomed to inmates turning down company.
He turned around and held up a flattened palm, signaling that the approaching footsteps stop.

Mindful of his instruction, the footsteps halted.

"I'm ill," I mouthed, rolling onto my side. Then I listened as he retreated away from the door.

"I'm sorry," he said; and, for a second, I thought he was apologizing to me.
But then a familiar voice asked, "What's going on?"

In response, the guard told her, "He said he's ill." Then, before Alexa could get a word in, he clarified, "But a lot of guys say this after waking up from a wet dream. It's easier than having to get out of bed with a semen stain on your pajama pants."

And with that, both pairs of footsteps trotted away and   left   me   in   silence.

Note of Appreciation

This book was published using Amazon's KDP service, so, I was unsure whether the subject matter would flag the attention of a digital or human moderator, rendering it unpublishable.

You can say what you like about Jeffrey P. Bezos, but I'd like to thank him for pioneering a service that lets an idiot like me write a first-person story about his life.

Freedom of speech might feel like an inalienable right, but only because the likes of Bezos uphold it.

About the Author

James.O.Hands is the author of '*Lasagne Police*' and '*Sauna Man*', and a part of the 83%.

Follow him on Twitter:
    https://twitter.com/JamesOHands
Instagram:
    https://www.instagram.com/james.o.hands/
Subscribe on YouTube:
    https://www.youtube.com/user/jamesohands
And join his Substack:
    https://jamesohands.substack.com

Thank you to r_sngr for the amazing graphic of Jeff Bezos as Santa Claus on the front cover.

Check him out on Instagram:
https://www.instagram.com/r_sngr/?hl=en